Acknowledgments
The author, illustrator and publisher would like to thank Irvine Carvery, Terry
Dixon, Coleman Howe, Gary Steed, Brenda Steed-Ross and Beatrice Wilkins,
former residents of Africville, for kindly reviewing the text and illustrations. The
author would also like to thank Africville descendant Suzy Hansen for her assis-
tance contacting former residents.

Photo credits (page 32, counterclockwise from top left)
From Africville, looking out to sea, 1964; Library and Archives Canada/Credit:
Ted Grant/Ted Grant fonds/e010750279.
Two Africville children, with Seaview African United Baptist Church and houses
behind it in the distance, Bob Brooks, photographer, ca. 1965; NSA, Bob Brooks
fonds, 1989-468 vol. 16 (scan 200715044).
Boys beside Canadian National railcar, Africville, with "Please boil this water
before drinking and cooking" sign in foreground, Bob Brooks, photographer,
ca. 1965; NSA Bob Brooks fonds, 1989-468 vol. 16/neg. sheet 18 image 37 (scan
200715055).

Source notes (page 32)
For more than … service. Africville Heritage Trust, 2012. africvillemuseum.org.
"the razing … compensation." "Former Africville residents want compensation,
and an apology," CBC News, July 24, 2004, cbc.ca.

To Tyshana.
— SG

To Ivory Tatem and
Gabriel Fortier-Campbell.
— EC

Groundwood Books / House of Anansi Press
groundwoodbooks.com

We acknowledge for their financial support of our publishing program the Canada
Council for the Arts, the Ontario Arts Council and the Government of Canada.

 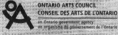

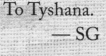

With the participation of the Government of Canada
Avec la participation du gouvernement du Canada | Canadä

Library and Archives Canada Cataloguing in Publication
Grant, Shauntay, author
Africville / Shauntay Grant ; [illustrated by] Eva Campbell.
Issued in print and electronic formats.
ISBN 978-1-77306-043-9 (hardcover). — ISBN 978-1-77306-044-6 (PDF)
I. Campbell, Eva, illustrator II. Title.
PS8613.R3663A63 2018   jC813'.6   C2018-900634-X
C2018-900635-8

The illustrations were done in oil and pastel on canvas.
Design by Michael Solomon
Printed and bound in Malaysia

AFRICVILLE

Shauntay Grant

Pictures by Eva Campbell

Groundwood Books
House of Anansi Press
Toronto   Berkeley

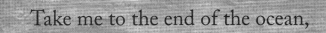

Take me to the end of the ocean,

where waves come to rest
and hug the harbor stones,

where the grass runs high up the hillside
and the houses lay out like a rainbow,

where home
smells like
sweet apple pie
and blueberry duff.

Take me up over the hill,
where the berries are thick
and tasty,

then meet me
at the Caterpillar Tree.
From there we'll run
Back the Field for football,

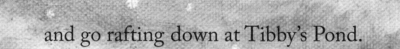
and go rafting down at Tibby's Pond.

Catch me a codfish, then come
watch the sea bring us all its treasures,

then take me to warm summer nights
down at Kildare's Field,
a bonfire burning red
like the going-down sun.

Take me to where the sky turns
purple and rose in the morning,
and light makes the salt water sparkle
like diamonds and stars.

Take me to where the pavement ends
and family begins,

OTHER EARLY
FAMILIES

where my great-grandmother's name
is marked in stone,

where stories are shared
all around me, the old songs
still quietly singing,

where memories turn to dreams,
and dreams turn to hope,
and hope never ends.

Take me …

to AFRICVILLE.

Africville was a Black community located on the shores of the Bedford Basin in Halifax, Nova Scotia. Its population peaked at around four hundred people, and the majority of its residents were landowners. Many Africville residents could trace their roots back to the arrival of Black Loyalists who migrated to Nova Scotia in the late 1700s during the American Revolutionary War, and Black Refugees who fled slavery in America during the War of 1812.

For more than 150 years, Africville was a vibrant, self-sustaining community that thrived in the face of opposition. Even though residents paid municipal taxes, they lived without services afforded other areas, such as running water, sewers and paved roads. They had no police, fire truck or ambulance service. As the City of Halifax grew, Africville became a preferred site for all kinds of unpleasant facilities — a slaughterhouse, a hospital for infectious diseases, and even the city garbage dump.

Instead of providing for the community, Halifax city officials decided to demolish Africville in the 1960s. Residents were moved out in city dump trucks, and their homes were destroyed. Many residents were relocated to public housing. But even though they were scattered, the community's determination to come together remained strong. In 1983, Africville residents returned to the shores of the Bedford Basin to host the first Africville reunion festival. The festival has since become an annual event that attracts former Africville residents and their families, friends and supporters.

In 2002, Africville was declared a National Historic Site of Canada. In 2004, a United Nations draft report stated that "the razing of Africville deserved compensation." Six years later, the City of Halifax offered an official apology to former Africville residents. As part of a compensation deal, a replica of the community's church was built on its original site, and the building now operates as a museum.

FOR FURTHER INFORMATION

africvillemuseum.org
A website that provides a wide range of information about Africville.

The Children of Africville by Christine Welldon, Nimbus Publishing, 2009.
A nonfiction book for young readers, with photographs.

The Spirit of Africville, Second Edition, by the Africville Genealogy Society, with contributions from Donald Clairmont, Stephen Kimber, Bridglal Pachai and Charles Saunders, Formac Publishing, 2010.
The story of Africville for older readers, including photographs.

Remember Africville, directed by Shelagh Mackenzie, National Film Board of Canada / CBC, 1991.
https://www.nfb.ca/film/remember_africville
A short documentary film about Africville.